The Golden Dreydl

The Golden Dreydl

Ellen Kushner

Illustrations by Ilene Winn·Lederer

ini Charlesbridge

Hanukkah

To my mom, who taught me Hebrew; my dad, who read me
The Thirteen Clocks; and Uncle Ron, who told me the jokes, this
book is lovingly dedicated—E. K.

With love and appreciation to my family, who are my past, present,
and future—I. W.-L.

Text copyright © 2007 by Ellen Kushner
Illustrations copyright © 2007 by Ilene Winn-Lederer
All rights reserved, including the right of reproduction in whole or in part in any form.
Charlesbridge and colophon are registered trademarks of Charlesbridge Publishing, Inc.

The Golden Dreydl was originally developed with Shirim Klezmer Orchestra under
the auspices of WGBH Radio Boston, and first appeared in different form as a radio
production of PRI's *Sound & Spirit with Ellen Kushner,* produced by WGBH Radio
Boston and distributed by PRI, Public Radio International.

Published by Charlesbridge
85 Main Street
Watertown, MA 02472
(617) 926-0329
www.charlesbridge.com

Library of Congress Cataloging-in-Publication Data
Kushner, Ellen.
    The golden dreydl / Ellen Kushner ; illustrated by Ilene Winn-Lederer.
        p. cm.
    Summary: After receiving a magic dreydl at Aunt Leah's Chanukah party, Sara is
catapulted into an alternate world of demons, fools, sorcerers, and sages.
    ISBN 978-1-58089-135-6 (reinforced for library use)
    [1. Hanukkah—Fiction. 2. Dreidel (Game)—Fiction. 3. Fairy tales.] I. Winn-Lederer,
Ilene, ill. II. Title.
PZ8.K965Go 2007
[Fic]—dc22   2006021257

Printed in the United States of America
(hc) 10 9 8 7 6 5 4 3 2 1

Illustrations created with pen, ink, watercolor, and digital media on
    Stonehenge archival paper
Display type handlettered by the illustrator after Queensland, designed by
    The Scriptorium, and text type set in Sabon
Printed and bound by Lake Book Manufacturing, Inc.
Production supervision by Brian G. Walker
Designed by Susan Mallory Sherman

The Golden Dreydl

Chapter 1

Iᴛ ᴡᴀꜱ ᴛʜᴇ ʜᴏʟɪᴅᴀʏ ꜱᴇᴀꜱᴏɴ, but Sara was not happy. Riding home from school on the bus was pure torture. Sara stared out the window at all the colored lights decorating the houses on street after street. . . . Sometimes people left their curtains open, and Sara could see right into their living rooms, where big trees glittered and shone.

Her friend Felicity poked her. "Here comes my stop. Are you coming to Trina's tomorrow? We're making Christmas cookies."

"Can't," Sara said glumly. "Family stuff."

"OK, I'll save you some. See you Monday!"

Felicity got off the bus in a flurry of red scarf and green coat. Sara could see Felicity's house beyond her, all decked out in giant candy canes, with reindeer landing on the roof next to a huge star blinking on and off.

When she got to her own house, it just looked dark and ordinary. She banged the front door loud enough for her mother to hear from the kitchen.

"Is that you, Sara? Don't drop your coat on the floor."

Sara dragged her coat into the kitchen and dropped it on a chair. She said to her mother, "I bet we're the only family on the block that doesn't have a Christmas tree!"

Sara's mother sighed. "You know we can't have a tree, honey; we're Jewish. Jews don't celebrate Christmas, so Jews don't have Christmas trees. End of story."

Sara knew her mother loved beautiful things. "But they're *beautiful*."

"I know, honey. And you can go over to your friends' houses and enjoy their trees as much as you like."

"It's not the same! *We're* not the same. Jews are weird."

Her mother stopped what she was doing and

crouched down in front of her, hands on her shoulders, and looked into her eyes. "Sara. Has someone said anything at school? Anything bad about being Jewish?"

"Mom, quit it. It's not like that. I just want a tree, that's all. Why can't we just have the same stuff as everyone else for once?"

"Sweetheart, we may not have an evergreen in our living room, but we have plenty of lights this time of year, now that Chanukah's started."

Sara kicked the floor sulkily. "Just eight dumb candles. So what? Chanukah's not even a very important Jewish holiday. You said so yourself."

"Maybe not. But it's what we celebrate in December, so learn to love it. SETTTHHH!!!" Sara's big brother Seth came barreling down the stairs, sounding like a herd of elephants, as their dad used to say. He wasn't much older than she was, but he was a whole lot bigger—especially his feet.

"What, Mom? I was just getting to the ninth level—" Seth liked computer games. He didn't care much about trees or lights if they weren't on a screen.

"Did you do your homework? Wash your face! Get changed, and go get your overnight bag. We're leaving for

Aunt Leah's in twenty minutes." Their mother opened the fridge and started taking out covered dishes. "It's the Chanukah party tonight, remember? What did we do with all the presents I wrapped? Sara, go get your sleepover bag."

"I'm not going," said Sara.

"Yaay!" Seth shouted.

Their mother ignored this. "Oh, yes you are. Come on, Sara, you know you always love Aunt Leah's Chanukah party. We'll eat latkes and light candles and sing songs and play dreydls. . . ."

"Dreydls are boring," said Sara.

"That's just 'cause you don't know how to play," said Seth.

"I do so!"

"Get your stuff and get in the car, kids," sighed their mother. "We'll be late!" She said that every year. And she was right.

Chapter 2

At Aunt Leah's party, the Chanukah candles had already been lit. The menorahs were sparkling in the windows, and the rooms were full of aunts and uncles and cousins of all ages, doing what they always did. The teenage cousins were off in a corner talking about teenage stuff, so everyone ignored them. The baby cousins were falling down and sticking their hands in the food, but everyone thought they were adorable anyway. Seth and Sara found their cousins Jason and Amy and Max, and they did what they did every year, which was to try and find all the gold-covered chocolate coins that had been scattered around as decorations and hide them to eat when no one was looking. Everyone really wanted to watch Aunt Leah's giant new plasma screen TV, but, "No TV at a family party!" said the grown-ups.

It was cold outside, but inside there was none of the crisp, snowy, green feeling that Sara loved at this time of year. Everything at the Chanukah party was warm and golden: the glowing candles, the deep-fried latkes, the applesauce, and the bright foil on the chocolate coins. . . . It was pretty, in its own way, and the food was fantastic as always. But it wasn't the same as at her friends' houses, with their evergreen wreaths and plaid ribbons, or at the mall with its candy-cane decorations, or the city department store windows with their scenes of Ye Olde Village with the carolers and the mistletoe. . . .

"Wake up, Sara!" said Seth. "How much chocolate have you got?"

Sara counted her coins. "Six big ones and five little ones."

"OK. Let's say the big ones are worth three little ones."

"Why?" she asked suspiciously. "I'm not giving you any."

"Of course you're not giving me any," he said loudly, as if he were talking to an idiot, "you're going to *play* me for them!" Jason and Amy laughed. "Told you she was sleeping," he said to them, and to Sara, "Told you you didn't know how to play dreydls."

"I do so!"

"OK, how?"

"You spin them around and you win stuff."

"Yeah, right," said Cousin Jason. He was Sara's age, but he was always trying to act big like Seth. "Don't they teach you anything in Hebrew School?" He thought he knew so much because he went to Hebrew School four days a week after school, while Seth and Sara only went on Sunday mornings.

"All right, everyone!" Uncle Isaac stood up, and everyone started clinking their spoons on glasses. They did this every year. It meant he was going to make a speech about how wonderful it was that they could all be together, and he did. The children waited patiently until he was done—then, before anyone could nab them and ask them how they liked school this year, they fled off together to a corner of the den. Amy produced a handful of little plastic dreydls and dumped them onto the floor.

Sara wasn't sure she really wanted to do this, but it was either join Seth and her cousins, or go off by herself and risk having grown-ups tell her how much they'd hated having their cheeks pinched when they were little and then try and pinch her cheek, not to mention asking, "So how's school?" . . . so she sat.

"Four sides." Seth picked up the biggest dreydl and showed it to all of them. "Four chances. OK, now everyone put a chocolate coin into the middle."

"Little or big?" Max needed to know. He was just a kid, not much more than a baby, but they had to let him play with them or they'd get in trouble.

"Big. OK, everyone in? I'll go—no, Amy, you go first," Seth said diplomatically. "Alphabetical order."

Cousin Amy was a good dreydl spinner. She gave it a twist in the air, then dropped it onto the floor. Around and around the little dreydl went; they had to scramble out of the way when it spun toward their knees because nobody wanted to stop it or it wouldn't count. Finally it fell over on its side. One Hebrew letter lay faceup.

"*Gimel.*" Amy read the letter. "That's a *gimel*. What do I get?"

"Um . . . *gimel's* good," Seth said. "I think it means— I think it means you get the whole thing."

"Great!" Amy scooped up all the coins. "Let's keep going. Everyone put a little one in."

"I don't wanna give her my chocolate!" Max whined.

"Don't be such a baby, Max."

"*Mo-o-o-o-o-o-omm—*"

"Shush!" Sara put her hand over Max's mouth. The last thing she wanted was Max and Amy's mother, Aunt Rachel, coming down on them and giving them yet another lecture on being nice to him because he was little. "Look, Max, you don't have to play with chocolate. You can play with nuts." There were always big bowls of nuts still in their shells at the Chanukah party, waiting for someone to get bored enough or hungry enough to crack them. Sara put a handful in front of him. She saw Jason opening his mouth to say it wasn't fair, but then he realized it wasn't worth it. Anyhow, it was his turn next. He spun, and the dreydl tottered and fell over immediately.

"Not fair—I get to do over."

"Wait, what did you get?"

They looked at the letter lying faceup. "*Nun*. That's like *none*; you don't get anything."

"I wanna do over. That didn't count."

"You can't," said Amy. "It's Max's turn. *Just put a little one in*," she muttered, then changed to her big-sister voice. "Come on, Maxie, spin the dreydl."

Max twisted the dreydl, and it fell on its side.

"Does that count?"

"It counts," Seth said quickly. "What'd you get, Max? Ohhh, *hey*. That's a good one."

"Daddy says 'Hay is for horses,'" Max said primly.

"This is a different *hey*—this is a Hebrew letter. It's like half. You get half of what's there."

Max scooped up all his nuts plus one coin. No one corrected him.

"What about the rest?"

"It stays in the pot," said Seth, like a poker player. It made the game seem more grown-up and interesting. "My turn. And I say—put in five."

"Wait a second," said Amy. "Since when did "e" come before "a"? I thought we were taking turns alphabetically. It's Sara's turn, not Seth's."

"I don't care," Sara muttered. Seth was always going on about how being older meant he got to do everything first. *Fine,* she thought. *Just finish the stupid game.*

And of course, because she wasn't arguing, Seth opened his mouth to be nice about it—but before he could say anything, Sara snatched up one of her two big coins and two of her little ones and threw them in the center. "Just go," she said. "OK?" The other cousins put in their five, too (except Max, who put in three nuts and got away with it). *The littlest and the biggest,* Sarah thought, *always get away with everything.*

Seth held the dreydl upside down in one hand, spun it, and flipped it at the last minute.

"Show-off," Sara muttered. It gave a quick bounce on the floor, like a stone skipping on a pond, and spun for a while before landing with the letter *shin* facing up.

"Aw, shoot," Seth grumbled.

"Give it up!" Jason crowed. "Come on, Seth, put one in. You gotta, when you get *shin.* That's the rule."

Seth tossed one of his coins into the middle. There were twenty-five chocolates in the pot, thirteen big and twelve small ones, and it was Sara's turn.

It might have been all right if Seth had kept his mouth shut. But Seth hated losing when he played games. Losing made him mean.

"Sara's going to spin, now," he said. "She's the baddest dreydl-spinner on the block. She's the Spin Queen of Dreydl Land. They call her 'Sara the Terra.' Come on, Sara, spin that thang!"

That did it. Sara put the dreydl down. "I'm not playing," she said.

"Why not?" asked Amy.

"This is a dumb game. It's a baby game."

"No, it's not," said Jason. "It's Jewish."

Amy said, "You're just saying that because you've only got five coins left."

"No, I'm not. I'm saying it because it's dumb."

"It's not dumb," Amy answered doggedly. Amy was a big fan of reason and logic. "You're just scared to lose."

"No, I'm not. Who cares, anyway? I said I'm not playing." Sara started scooping up what was left of her coins.

"You were playing when you put your chocolate in," Jason said. "Don't you want to try and win it back?"

"Nope. I said I don't care. Dreydls are boring."

Amy was cautious and reasonable, except for when

she wasn't. Sometimes she'd just cut loose and surprise you. "OK," Amy said, "let's make it interesting." Everyone watched with their mouths open as Amy threw all her chocolate coins into the middle—the big ones and the little ones.

"That's everything," she said. "I'm betting everything, and everyone else has to, too. The next *gimel* takes them all. It's your turn, Sara."

It was a dare, and they knew it. The coins came pouring into the center: five more, ten more, eighteen more. . . . The pile glittered with chocolate and promise, and Sara wondered what it would be like to scoop them all up. All she had to do was back down. All she had to do was pick up the dreydl and spin. . . .

"Come on, Sara!"

"I—"

"Sara, are you playing or not?"

"Sara, do it!"

All of a sudden, the front door blew open with a bang so loud they heard it across the house. "*Hag sameach!*" a high voice shouted, almost as loud as the door.

Max jumped. "What's that?"

"Hebrew for 'Happy Holiday,'" Jason explained.

"But who *is* that? What's all the noise?" The grown-ups were calling to each other, sounding surprised and glad. "Everyone's already here, aren't they? Aunt Rachel and Uncle Izzy," he counted, "Aunt Sophie and Uncle Abe. Uncle Joseph and Aunt Colleen, Great-Aunt Chaya and Dr. Maimon, all the Springhill cousins, plus Ruth and Naomi and their evil twins who never stop screaming. Oh, and us. So who's missing?"

They ran to the door to see.

It was an old, old lady, with a huge old satchel on her shoulders. Her hair was as white as the moon, and she was all wrapped up in layers and layers of scarves, scarves like all the colors of the world.

"*Chanukah alegre!*" she cried, "and a *gut yontif* to you all. *Buen moed,* everyone. May the oil in your lamp never run out!"

"Who *is* that?" Jason whispered, and many of the uncles seemed to be asking the same thing. But Sara's mother and the other aunts had huge wondering smiles on their faces, as if a combination of Gandalf and Mary Poppins had just walked in the door.

"I don't believe it," Aunt Leah said.

"It's Tante Miriam, after all these years!"

Sara's mother and aunts rushed forward to help the old woman. "Tante Miriam!" They clustered around her, taking off scarves and kissing her and peppering her with hugs and questions. "Auntie, how are you? Do you remember me? Tante Miriam, where've you been? And how on earth did you get here?"

"You may well ask!" The old lady shook herself free of her scarves. "It's been some trip! Deserts, mountains, rivers . . . I crossed the Red Sea with all the rest. On the shore I danced, and then I sang and beat my drum and tambourine. . . . And then I collected a few things—you know, for the children. C'm'ere, children!"

The kids couldn't help drawing closer. It was a very big bag the old lady was carrying. Out of it came wonderful things: costumes and candy, sailboats and dump trucks, glitter and spangles and paint sets and drums. It was as if the old woman knew what each of them wanted, without ever having met them. Amy got the telescope she'd been dying for. Jason got an antique baseball autographed by Sandy Koufax. Seth got a complete set of enamel paint for his character models, and Max got a toy pirate ship, plus a bandana and eyepatch. Everybody got something. . . . Finally, only Sara was left.

"For you," said Tante Miriam, "for you, my girl, I have something verrrry special." She reached into the bottom of the bag, and handed Sara—a Chanukah dreydl. A shiny, gold metal dreydl, almost as big as a book.

"Oh." Sara had been taught that if you didn't act grateful for every present, no matter what it was, you were never going to get any more. But it was hard to hide her disappointment. "Thank you," she said glumly. She stood there holding the oversize dreydl, feeling like the world's biggest idiot.

"Hey, let's play!" Her brother grabbed the golden dreydl out of her hands.

"Quit it!" Sara said automatically. But Seth and the other cousins spun it all over the living room, yelling and grabbing and laughing.

"Watch out, you kids!" cried the grown-ups. Seth and the others weren't really trying to play the dreydl game, they were just showing off how far they could make it spin before it fell down. The dreydl was heavy, with fancy squiggles and scrollwork all over, like a work of art, not a toy. You were probably supposed to keep it on a shelf on display and not play with it at all. It took both hands to hold and spin. But the grown-ups didn't try to stop them, because it was Chanukah and they were supposed to be glad that the children were playing with a real Chanukah toy and not some plastic piece of junk or video game. "Don't hurt the furniture!"

In the middle of the chaos, the lights flickered and the room grew dim. It was old Tante Miriam, lifting her arms above them all.

"Wait!" she said. As if by magic, everyone stopped at once. Even the teenagers took out their earbuds, and the grown-ups put down their drinks to listen to her.

"Chanukah is a time for joy," Tante Miriam said. "But dreydls, you know, have their rules. They have their time and their season. And there are four sides to every dreydl." The grown-ups nodded, but she ignored them, her face turned toward the children. "What is written on those sides?"

"Letters," said Cousin Amy.

"But which letters are they?"

"Hebrew letters," Cousin Jason said quickly, because he had to know more than anyone. "*Nun, gimel, hey, shin.*"

"Letters that begin the words *Nes Gadol Haya Sham*:

A Great Miracle Was There. So be careful how you spin that dreydl, children, for with it you are spinning miracles." A baby started to cry and was rocked and hushed. "If your dreydl lands on the side with the letter *gimel*, you win all you can see before you—but whether or not that is for the best, who knows? Unless you can see the next spin, and the one beyond that, never be too sure. . . . For hear me well: it is in the nature of dreydls to spin, as it is in the nature of the world to change. On *hey*, you give half and keep half—so be sure you have something worth keeping. And try to give with a generous heart. *Nun* means nothing, no change at all; things remain as they were. Not always a bad thing, not really. And if your dreydl lands on the letter *shin*, it means loss. You must give up something precious, maybe the one thing you cherish most. But never fear to spin again—for maybe it was something you needed to lose in the first place."

Now the whole room was looking at Sara's present.

"Cool," breathed Seth, balancing the dreydl on one hand. "And what if you—"

"That's mine," Sara said loudly.

"What?"

"That's my present," she said. "Give it."

"Nuh-uh." Seth slung it behind his back like a basket-ball. "You didn't even want it."

"Who says?" It might be just a dumb dreydl, but it was *her* dumb dreydl! "I didn't say you could play with it."

"It's mine now. By right of conquest and eminent domain."

Sara didn't shout "Mo-om!" She just went for him. She got her hands on the dreydl, but her brother grabbed it back and held it up high over her head. Sara jumped, and jumped again. She knocked it right out of his hand, and—and—then it happened.

The dreydl went flying—up in the air, right into Aunt Leah's giant TV screen. There was a horrible sound, as if a hundred screaming cats were being tortured. And then there was silence.

The screen was cracked from top to bottom.

"Oh. My. God." Sara's mother was white-faced. "Leah, I am so sorry—"

"Hey," said Aunt Leah quietly, trying to sound cheer-ful and not quite succeeding, "don't worry about it, Becky. We watch too much TV as it is."

Aunt Rachel was on the warpath. "See what happens?! See what happens when you kids get wild?"

Max started crying. Sara had to bite the inside of her cheek to keep from doing it, too.

"Nice going, Sara," Seth muttered.

"That's enough, kids!" Their mother clapped her hands once. "Bed. Right now. All of you."

Jason complained, "*We* didn't do anything. It was Seth and Sara—"

She just glared at him.

"But what about presents?" Amy asked in a small voice. "We haven't opened family presents yet."

Aunt Leah said softly, "Maybe tomorrow, kids. Good night."

Chapter 3

SARA COULDN'T SLEEP. No one was speaking to her, not even Amy. It was not fair. Sara knew it was not fair. She hadn't meant to throw the dreydl at the TV. All she'd wanted was to get it away from Seth. But when she touched it, it had seemed to fly from her hand like a rocket, shot right into the screen for a landing.

Maybe the damage wasn't as bad as it looked. Maybe they could fix it. Maybe she could sell the dreydl to help pay for the TV. What if it were real gold? It was still her present, wasn't it? "Something verrrry special," Tante

Miriam had said. Maybe she meant it was worth thousands of dollars! If Sara sold it, she could buy giant TVs for everyone, maybe.

"Hey, Amy," Sara whispered from the bunk bed below her cousin. Usually they tossed for who got the top bunk, but this time Amy had just taken it without asking.

"Shut up!" hissed one of the teenage cousins, who was on the floor in a sleeping bag.

"I'm going to the bathroom," Sara muttered. She pulled on her slippers and grabbed her robe and crept downstairs to the living room. The rooms downstairs smelled of burned-out fires, the way they always did after all the candles in the menorahs had burned down to nothing and put themselves out. The house was dark. Even the grown-ups had gone to bed.

There was a glow of light in the living room, though—and it seemed to be coming from the busted TV. Sara breathed out a gentle *phew!* Maybe the TV wasn't really broken after all. In fact, she was almost sure it wasn't, because she could hear voices coming from it. Some sort of adventure program was on, with people shouting, "Come on! Hurry up! Are you coming through or not?"

The light and the voices guided her into the living

room. Sara stared at the screen. Had the TV always been this big? It was nearly as tall as she was. But the crack was still there, so bright she could hardly look at it. And there was no program on, nothing to see at all—nothing but the voices, calling, calling:

"Come on! Hurry up! Tante Miriam crossed the Red Sea—are you scared to follow through here?"

She stared at the crack getting higher—as high as a door—as high as the wall, growing, growing. . . .

"Come on, girl, don't be a chicken!"

Sara took a step toward the screen.

She stepped on something squishy that moved under her.

"Yeow!" a new voice cried. "That hurt!"

In the dazzling light Sara saw a girl her own age on the floor—a girl with crazy golden hair and sparkling eyes.

"Help me up," the girl gasped. "We've got to get through before it closes!"

The girl gripped her arm, and Sara hauled her to her feet.

"Come on," the girl said, pulling Sara toward the TV. "Aren't you coming? Don't you want to see?"

"But it's broken," Sara said wildly, trying to get free.

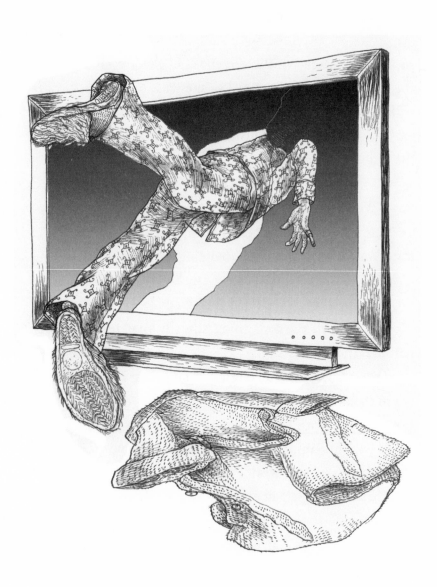

"No, it's not—it's finally fixed!" And with that, the girl hurled herself into the golden light, taking Sara with her.

Sara heard music, or maybe it was just voices, the voices of hundreds of people, all calling to her to follow them . . . then it became a crystal sound, like wine glasses ringing when you wet the rims, only many, so many, deep and rich and high and clear. . . .

Chapter 4

NEXT THING SHE KNEW, Sara found herself sprawled in the green grass of a meadow, the golden girl at her side. It was daytime, sunny and warm. There were yellow flowers everywhere, and it smelled like summer vacation. Off in the distance, majestic mountains stretched purple into the clouds, but above them the sky was a perfect blue.

"How did you land?" the girl asked breathlessly. "Did you win or lose?"

"Huh?"

The girl got up and brushed herself off. "Didn't you look? How did you fall?"

"I—don't know," Sara said, confused. "I'm OK, I guess. I mean, I'm fine."

"You'll find out later," the girl said. "That's for sure. I fell on *gimel*. I win!"

"How do you know?"

"I'm lucky that way."

It wasn't an answer, but Sara didn't care so much about *how* she landed as *where*. "Where are we?"

"We're home!" the girl said happily.

"This isn't *my* home."

"Why not? It could be. You can live anywhere, really, if you put your mind to it. I've lived in your world for years."

"But—what were you doing at Aunt Leah's? What happened to the TV? Who are you, anyway?"

The girl grinned. "Don't you recognize me?" She lifted her arms over her head and spun around until she fell, dizzy and laughing, onto the grass. "That's a *hey*, Sara: you only get to keep half of what you got—'cause I'm your special gift—your golden dreydl!" She was certainly gifted

at spinning and falling. "You can be my friend, though, and that's a thing worth keeping. Get it?"

No, Sara wanted to say, *I don't get it at all.* But what good would it do? This girl seemed so fizzy, no matter what—dizzily, giddily happy, as if she knew everything were a big joke, and she knew the punchline, and Sara didn't, but Sara was supposed to, and she was dumb not to get it.

"Right," Sara said. "You're a dreydl, and I'm—" Then she saw it, a deep red scratch on the dreydl girl's arm. "Hey," said Sara, "you're hurt."

The girl put her hand over the scratch. "No, I'm not. I'm fine. I'm home, and I'm just fine."

Sara fished in her pajama pocket and pulled out a tissue. Her pockets were always lumpy with them, and her mother complained that they got all disgusting in the wash when she forgot to take them out first. But this time it was a good thing they were there, because the girl really was bleeding all down her arm. Sara pressed a couple to the scratch. "Hold this," she instructed. "Press down really hard; it'll stop the blood."

The girl stared at her own arm. "Wow," she said. "I

guess I got wounded when you threw me at the big screen."

"When I *what*?! I didn't throw you anywhere—you know I didn't!"

"You did, Sara, you know you did," the girl said helpfully, as if she were reminding her of a candy bar she'd dropped. "You got mad at your brother 'cause he was having fun and you weren't, and he held me up in the air and you grabbed me and threw me and—"

"Hold it," said Sara. "You weren't there."

"Yes, I was, I told you."

Sara took a deep breath. She had a feeling she knew where this was going—but she didn't want this girl to get away with it so easily. "OK. So you were a big, golden dreydl, and Tante Miriam brought you in her bag."

"That's right," the girl said nodding encouragingly.

"So how do you know everything that happened?" Sara asked logically. "Dreydls don't have any ears. Or any eyes."

The girl gave her a look like she was being truly dumb. "I'm not *really* a dreydl," she said. "I was just *being* one."

Sara sighed. She'd always prayed for magic to be real some day, but she hated stories where it just happened for no reason or didn't make sense. "OK, let's say you were being this big, metal dreydl, but you're really a girl—but at the *time*, you were a dreydl, right?"

The girl nodded, her wiry golden curls splashing her neck.

"So how did you get a cut on your arm, huh?"

"I *told* you."

Sara was glad to see the other girl looking confused, for once. She moved in to make her point. "I mean, it's like 'Rock, Paper, Scissors,'" Sara went on. "Metal cracks glass. Glass doesn't scratch metal."

"I'm not metal," the girl said mournfully.

"But then how did you get wounded? Cause you were still a dreydl then, right?"

The girl just started spinning around. She was wearing a thin dress made of many layers of fine material: green, yellow, a little blue, a little red . . . like the colors you see in a candle flame. She spun herself into dizziness, then fell into the soft grass. She looked up at Sara. "Oops," she said. She wasn't laughing now. "That's a *shin*."

"Loss," Sara said. "But it's only a game." This was

starting to spook her. She knew perfectly well none of this was normal. And it wasn't "just a dream," either. She never had dreams like this. It was like a story in a book, or a movie. Wherever she was, she didn't belong here, and she didn't know the rules. And no amount of logical thinking or arguing with this girl was going to change that. "It's only a game, right?"

"Are you playing?" the girl asked. She looked serious for once. She looked right into Sara's eyes, and her eyes were blue like the heart of a flame. "Are you playing? 'Cause if you're not playing, you have to get out."

I'm not playing. She'd said it once already that night. But that was different. That was Seth and Amy and everyone being stupid to her. Here, she was all alone, except for her "special gift," the golden dreydl that weird Tante Miriam had pulled last out of the bag for her.

"I'm playing," Sara said. "What do I have to do?"

"Spin," the girl said.

"But—" Sara felt like it would just be so dumb. She hadn't spun around like that since she was a little kid. "But—I'm not a dreydl!" she objected.

"Neither am I!" the girl sang out. She stuck out her arms at both sides, like Sara and Seth used to do when they were playing airplane. And the smell of the grass under her feet was the smell of long summer afternoons with nothing to do but turn around and around until the trees went round and round overhead. Sara spun. Sara spun, and Sara laughed. Her voice was loud and silly, and the dreydl girl's voice joined hers like one bird in a tree calling to another that something good had come into their world. She spun until she had to fall down, and she was still laughing when she flopped down onto the sweet, sweet grass.

"How did you land?" the girl asked, lying beside her.

"Um . . ." Sara looked down at her panting belly, but she didn't see any letters there. "How can you tell?"

"Practice, practice, practice!" It sounded like one of those dopey jokes her father used to tell.

"No way," Sara said. "I don't think I'm cut out to be a dreydl. How did you land, yourself?"

The girl looked down. "*Nun.*" She frowned. "*Nun* means nothing. Let's try again."

"No more spinning. I want to do something different now. Let's go exploring, or get something to eat, or something. Does anyone else live here? Is this a magic world, or just Europe or something? Are there vampires? Do you have to go to school?"

The dreydl girl was picking at some of the blood that had dried on her arm. Then she looked up into the distance.

"Do you like adventures?" she asked.

"Sometimes. What kind?"

"Maybe one with demons?"

It sounded like one of Seth's computer games. "What kind of demons?"

The girl pointed with her chin toward the purple mountains. Off in the distance, a grayish cloud bristled with angry motion. The cloud was rushing closer and closer, so quickly that soon both girls could see the shape of huge beasts and hear the flap of wings. The weird thing was, they looked backward—it was a lot of tails and hooves and things, coming closer and closer. . . .

"What is it?" Sara whispered.

"Demons." For the first time, the dreydl girl's voice was tinged with fear. "Hordes of them—an entire demon army. I thought they were still locked up in Solomon's Cave!"

Sara gulped. "Well, they're not. What should we do?"

"If they're on the march, it means only one thing: the demons have escaped—and we'd better run and warn the king!"

They took off across the grass. Sara was a good runner, at least. But two girls, even fast ones, are no match for huge creatures with hooves and horns and wings, scaly and feathered and fast. In no time at all, the demons had them surrounded.

Greatest of them all, riding a fierce beast that was half-camel, half-goat, with fire breathing from his nostrils, was a demon in armor glittering with jewels and a crown on his head: the Demon King. He stared down at them with red eyes and lifted his hand high.

All of a sudden, the dreydl started to spin. For a second, Sara thought she was just being silly, or else trying to do her special magic—but then she saw her face. The dreydl girl looked so scared. Sara grabbed for her hand, but a powerful force was pulling her away.

"Help me, Sara!" cried her friend. Sara tried to hook her arm, but it slipped from her grasp as the dreydl turned faster and faster, like a dancer doing a million pirouettes, but clumsy, not elegant, trying to resist. And she wasn't just spinning in circles. She was moving closer and closer to the terrible creature whose hand was still raised, wielding an awful power.

The dreydl spun straight toward the Demon King. With a cry of triumph, the demons surrounded her and caught her in a giant net.

Sara was too mad to be scared. It shouldn't be this easy for them. She shouldn't be all alone with nothing to fight them with. They didn't pay any attention to her, as if she were not even there, as if she weren't really playing, like the kid nobody wanted on their team. They just loaded the dreydl girl across the back of one of their monstrous steeds, wheeled, and rode away.

"Come back!" cried Sara. But it was too late. The Golden Dreydl was in the hands of the Demon King's armies.

Chapter 5

SARA WATCHED HELPLESSLY as the demon army thundered off toward the mountains, with the Golden Dreydl bound fast. They went as they had come—backward. It should have been funny, but it wasn't at all. It was like watching a movie in reverse, when you know that it's going somewhere really awful. Soon there was nothing to see but a cloud of gray dust, and after that, nothing at all.

The sky was still blue, the grass green. The yellow flowers nodded in the warm breeze. Sara wondered if she should try spinning. But she wasn't sure what that really meant. Look what had happened last time! Had the drey-dl's spinning called the demons forth? Could Sara *un*spin what had just happened? Or would she only make things worse?

Maybe spinning just predicted what your fortune would be. . . . But did she really want to know?

"Oh, dear, dear, dear, and possibly even lackaday, if it comes to that." Sara whirled around to see a tall, stately woman, with skin the color of golden honey, standing right behind her. "Lost her already, have you?"

"I'm sorry," Sara gasped, startled out of her wits—*where had this woman come from?*—and uncomfortably aware of just who she was talking about. "It wasn't my fault—I couldn't help her, I tried!"

"Not good, child." The woman's voice was like honey, too, deep and slow and lovely. Her jet-black hair ran down her back in dozens of tiny braids, dotted with bells and bright beads. "I would say you'd lost your luck, but we're not done with the game yet. Now, think care-fully: how did she land this time, when they caught her?"

"I don't know. I couldn't see."

"Close your eyes," the woman said. "Try seeing that way."

"Right before they came, it was a *nun*—and before that, it was—it was *shin*."

The beautiful woman looked grave.

"That's bad, huh?" Sara couldn't stop talking, she was so nervous. Was it her fault, somehow? Would they lock her up? Or turn her into a menorah or something? "What will they do to her?"

"It's not so much what they will do to her, as what we will do without her."

"Um," Sara said, "who's *we*?"

"Forgive me." The woman raised one slender arm. The bracelets on it clattered and jingled. "I am Belkis, Queen of Sheba." She gestured behind her, and Sara saw that they were not alone: a string of camels, decked in tassels and striped cloth, with attendants and lots of baggage wrapped in more bright cloth, stretched out behind her. "I was journeying toward the Tree of Life," said the Queen, "to meet my husband, King Solomon the Wise. It was he who bound the Demon King in the first place—forever, we had hoped. Your little friend is our daughter, our beloved child—our youngest, and most rash."

This wise, proud queen is the dreydl's mother?! Sara thought, her heart sinking. *Am I in trouble now!*

"Did the—did the demons turn her into a dreydl?" Sara asked.

"Oh, no," the queen smiled. "Her father did that."

Sara wondered what the dreydl girl had done. Something pretty bad, she imagined—something a lot worse than not setting the table or not finishing her homework.

"At first, I did not like it," the queen said. "But you know how she is. It is so hard to say no to her."

"You mean, she *wanted* to be changed?"

"In a manner of speaking. She begged us both, day and night, to be allowed to travel to other worlds! I knew she was much too young—but Solomon could deny her nothing. And so King Solomon sealed her with four powerful magic letters, to keep her from harm. It was for her own protection, you see."

"It was?"

The queen nodded. "For a while she roamed free, tasting the customs of many different worlds, able to change at will if things got too much for her or danger threatened. Her father thought it was educational. But here at home, the demons were growing in strength."

Sara tried to look as if she understood. "They're evil, huh?"

"Evil? No. They come from the breath of the Creator, as we all do. Troublemakers are what they are. Demons love confusion. They love mistakes—especially other people's. A demon will trick you into your own worst self, if he can. And then you are in trouble indeed. Why, once King Solomon himself was tricked into—but please," the queen suddenly interrupted herself, "forgive me! I am so rude. You are a guest in our land. You have come a long way, longer than you know. It is unthinkable that I not offer you some refreshment."

She clapped her hands, and her attendants set out brass trays heaped with good things to eat and drink. There was rice mixed with nuts and raisins, and a yogurt smoothie drink that tasted like almonds. Sara's favorite was rice pudding with the smell of roses, sprinkled with flakes of real gold leaf. When they were done, attendants handed them little bowls of water scented with orange flowers to dip their fingers into, and fine linen napkins to dry them.

"That's better," the Queen of Sheba said.

Sara had to agree. But now that she was rested and

fed, her mind was full of questions. "What is this place?" Sara asked.

The queen smiled. "For us, it is home. And for you, too, Sara, for your roots are here with the Tree, and you live and learn among its many leaves."

"What tree?" Sara looked around the meadow.

"I get ahead of myself," said the queen. "Be patient with me, and you shall know what you need to know. Beginning with my daughter, who loves movement and change and who came to your world with just one thought: to run free in a place where the letters dance so quickly it is almost impossible to keep up with them. But her father and I had sent her there for a different reason: to keep her safe, so we need not worry while we worked hard to defeat the demons here."

Sara couldn't help wondering what sort of parents thought of her world as a safe place for a kid to run free. *It must be nice to be magic,* she thought.

The queen went on. "Long years we struggled against Ashmedai, the Demon King, and his minions, to bind them all in Solomon's Cave. At last the deed was done, and the time seemed right for our daughter to return. But over the years, the way had closed. We knew that she was there, but she could not get home! We did not know what to do. We were so glad that you were able to open the door, my dear!"

This was the first time a grown-up had thanked Sara for breaking the TV screen. She felt a little better. Maybe it was all going to be all right after all. If she'd failed to protect the Golden Dreydl from demons, at least she'd brought her home.

"How the demons escaped, I do not know." The queen shook her head with annoyance, like Sara's friend's mom wondering how the dog got out of the yard. "Perhaps the opening of the door set them free; a small price to pay for my daughter's return. But now that they are on the loose again, we must get her back!"

"But you said they wouldn't hurt her," Sara said anxiously. "And the magic letters, won't they keep her safe?"

"Those letters protect her, true. . . . But even more importantly, she is their keeper. You see, Solomon put great power into her. The four magical letters she is sealed with come from the Tree of Life. Do you know the Tree of Life, Sara?"

Sara thought of Shabbat services, when the Torah scroll was taken out and the rabbi held it up and said, "It is the tree of life of all who hold fast to it, and all its paths are peace."

"Is it a Torah?"

"That is one of its branches. You and my daughter are, too, and so is the entire alphabet, every letter in every language."

"I don't get it."

"The Tree is at the heart of everything, all learning and all creation. It is what has been and what is to come, the source of all that is good. In taking the power of those four letters from the tree and sealing them into our young daughter, Solomon was wise, as he is always wise . . . but also he took risks, as the wise sometimes must.

"Now she must return that power to the Tree—or the very heart of the world is lost. I do not fear for my daughter's life, or for her courage. But without the letters that our child carries, the Tree of Life itself may die, and all light and music, knowledge and wisdom slowly cease. It means an end to all growing things—an end to going forward. Demons like to go backward, for they do not like things to change and grow."

"Tell me more about the demons," Sara said. "I don't think there are any real ones in our world."

"There used to be," the queen said, "but they don't like petroleum by-products. I think they're—what do you call it? Allergistic?"

"Allergic," Sara told her. Well, that made sense. Lots of magical things that were in old stories didn't seem to be around much anymore. She wondered if fuel oil made demons break out in hives, or choke, or what? She wished she'd known. She could have brought some with her.

"Do you understand now, Sara?" the queen asked. "I am grateful to you for helping my daughter once. Will you help her, and us, again?"

"Why me?" Sara asked. "I mean, I'm just a kid. I'm not even magic."

"And that is why," the queen replied. "The demons do not know you. They don't know what you're made of. You are something new in the world."

"What do I have to do?"

"Come with me to the demon camp. I will send riders to warn King Solomon not to expect me right away. After that, we will see what we will see."

Sara said, more bravely than she felt, "Let's go, then."

"Thank you," said the queen. She took Sara's hand. "But first: I know you left home in a hurry. Perhaps a change of clothes would be useful?" Sara gratefully realized the Queen of Sheba was suggesting she get out of her pajamas. "I am sorry we do not have time to make new things for you, but perhaps these would fit." From one of the bags, the queen took loose trousers and a shirt of colored silk, with a vest and a cape to go with them, and boots of the softest leather, embroidered with flowers Sara had never seen before. The attendants surrounded her and helped her into her new things.

"Most becoming," the queen approved. "And now, please get up on one of my camels. We have a long way to go."

Chapter 6

RIDING A CAMEL was not as much fun as it looked. It was sort of uneven, like a car with a flat tire. And the leg Sara had hooked over the saddle horn got awfully stiff. The view was good, though.

They left the grasslands behind and soon were plodding through the desert. It seemed like hours since the queen's caravan passed through the beautiful land. Sara was so tired she was afraid she'd fall off her camel. She tried to think of exciting things, but her head started to nod. She was dreaming of spinning dreydls—and the next thing she knew, Sara found herself sitting on the ground, while the camels receded further and further into the distance.

"Hey!" Sara shouted. "Hey, I'm back here!" But nobody turned around. They couldn't hear her. Soon the camels were just tiny specks.

She got up, rubbing her legs.

"You poor child," said a voice behind her. "How you must be suffering."

She turned and saw a bird. Well, not just any bird: a *peacock*, a glorious splash of color on the desert landscape. Its blues were bluer than a summer sky, and the green and gold of its tailfeathers glowed like jewels at twilight. The peacock was talking to her. At home, birds didn't talk, except parrots, and they didn't know what they were saying. But this one did.

"You admire me," said the bird. "Anyone would. It is very natural, and nothing to be ashamed of. God made me to be admired. It's true—everyone else in the world has their work to do. Even God. But I do not."

"God *works*?" Sara asked, distracted by the thought.

"Of course. In the beginning, God worked very hard

to create the world. For six days and nights the Spirit breathed life into creation. Why else did the Creator need to rest on the seventh day?"

"So how come *you* don't work?"

"Ah." The peacock inclined its lovely head modestly. "Well. When God made all the animals and gave us our tasks, the Living One asked each of us what we would like. The horse asked for speed and strength to run; the leopard asked for keen smell and sharp claws to hunt.

"Then all the birds got started: the thrush wanted a sweet voice to soothe the heart, the chickens wanted lots of cute little eggs to lay. . . . By the time they got to me, what was left?

"'Creator of the Universe,' I said, 'you have made me according to your will. Isn't it enough that I be beautiful?'

"God laughed and said yes, that was enough if I thought it was. (I don't like being laughed at, but, after all, *God*, you know. . . .) Now," said the peacock, "don't you think I made the right choice? Wouldn't you want to be like me and just stand around and be admired?"

Sara considered it. "I don't think there's much anyone would admire about me," she said. "I'm not really beautiful or anything."

"Well . . ." The peacock tilted its tiny head. "You are still growing. But you are so gifted!" it hastened to add. "I bet you can whistle."

That was true. Sara could whistle really well—much better than Seth. It made him nuts. She could whistle part of a piece by Vivaldi with bird sounds in it that her mother really liked.

"Your friends pretend not to care, but they admire you for it, I'm sure," the peacock said.

"Would you like to hear me?" Sara asked, pursing her lips.

"Of course . . . but later, later."

Sara felt deflated. "I guess whistling isn't that big a deal after all, huh?"

"But that's not all, is it? Remember when you did the gymnastic routine with the handstand, and everyone applauded? They were admiring you then. You liked it, didn't you?" *Well, who wouldn't?* Sara remembered the glow she'd felt. "Work is nothing like that. No one admires you for just doing your job. How many times have you taken out the trash without even being thanked?"

It's true, Sara thought. *No matter how hard I work,*

it's never enough. The garbage still has to go out, the dishes still have to get cleaned. . . . I do homework and study, and it never ends. But if I could be like the peacock and just sit around doing nothing . . .

She was picturing it all so clearly, she didn't notice how the stranger arrived. But once he was there, he was hard to miss: he had a sock stuck on his head over his spiky bright red hair, and he wore a plaid jacket with an undershirt over it. His necktie was around his waist, and his shoes—well, one was a black-and-white leather oxford shoe, and the other was a purple sneaker with green laces. He didn't look like a clown, though. Sara hated clowns. He looked like someone who had gotten dressed in the dark on three separate days without ever checking a mirror.

The peacock ignored him, but the newcomer looked them both up and down. "Very nice," he said. "Ohhh, how I admire you! If I could just have a few feathers of your tail, my friend, I would have a nose-picker the entire world would envy! I'd be sitting there picking my nose with those feathers, and boy, how people would admire me!"

"As if I care," the peacock said.

"Now, you." The man turned to Sara. "You're the

real thing. I can always tell the genuine article. I admire you already. But I'd like to look up to you. There's only one problem—I can't do it from this angle. Any chance you can do a handstand?"

"Sure." But as soon as Sara stood on her hands, so did the little man.

"No, it's no good," he said, staring into her face. "We're still seeing eye to eye."

"I could stand up."

"No, wait, I think I've got it. . . ." The man reached for his own knee with one hand and fell over, rolling in the dust so his sock got stuck on his ear. Sara couldn't help it; she laughed.

"Are you admiring me?" he asked.

Sara scrambled to her feet, politely trying to hide her giggles. "Not exactly."

"Good! I'm bringing you pleasure—I'm making you laugh—and that's a lot more important! So let's go!"

"Wait a minute. . . ." Sara looked around for the elegant creature. But it was nowhere to be seen. "The peacock—it's gone!"

The newcomer waved his hand dismissively. "Of course it's gone. We weren't admiiiiiiiiiring it, so it took a

walk. See, that bird's not interested in you unless you're interested in it. It wouldn't take the trouble to tell you you were on fire if you had flames coming out of your ears."

"Is that so?" Sara said, a little annoyed. She'd thought the peacock was pretty nice, actually. Friendly, and sympathetic. This guy was—well, he certainly said whatever he was thinking. "And what about you?"

"You can trust me. I'm the Fool."

"You're a fool?"

"*The* Fool!" He pulled off his undershirt, scrubbing at the dust on his jacket with it. "There are plenty of fools in the world, but they don't do it full-time. And believe me, it takes work. It's my job to make people laugh, to turn the world upside down, to shake it and see what comes out. You know the old saying: 'Better to keep your mouth shut and let people *think* you're a fool, than to open it and let them know it'? Well, when I open my mouth, I sure let them *know* it! But I don't mind. How can you do any good in the world if you're always worried about what people might think of you? Just standing around being scared—it's almost as bad as going backward, like the demons!"

"Ohmigosh!" Sara cried. "I'm supposed to be chasing

the demon army and rescuing the Golden Dreydl!"

"Demons have captured King Solomon's daughter?" He waved his arms about, running around in tiny circles, kicking up sand. "We must get a move on! As quickly as possible! Without delay! This very minute—if not sooner!"

"But how do we find the demons?"

"How do we find the demons?" he repeated. "We *fool* them—by making them think we're going backward, like them!"

And he put his sock on his head backward and both shoes on his feet backward.

"Come on," he said, "follow me!"

Sara didn't even see a path, but the Fool rushed forward. "Come on," he repeated, "it's a shortcut!"

And there before them, suddenly, were bushes and trees and a path that hadn't been there before, and Sara was running down it.

Chapter 7

THE ROAD SEEMED TO SPIN BY—or maybe it was the Fool
who kept Sara's head spinning with his riddles and jokes.

"What is it," the Fool asked, "that makes you cry but
doesn't make you sad?"

She used to like riddles, but not anymore. Riddles
were babyish. And she'd never heard this one.

"You don't know?" said the Fool. "C'mon, it's an
easy one."

"I'm too old for riddles."

"*Whaaaaaaa?*" The Fool stopped dead in his tracks.
He stuck his finger in his ear and bulged his tongue out

inside his cheek and wiggled it around, so it looked like he was cleaning out the inside of his head. "Am I hearing what I think I'm hearing? Tell me I'm not hearing this thing that I think I'm hearing but really am not."

"Riddles are just for kids," Sara said stubbornly.

"Oy." The Fool shook his spiky red head. "Right. Kids like that Greek hero, Eddy Puss or something, who riddled at the crossroads with the Great Sphinx for his life and crown. Kids like the mighty Samson, who challenged an entire party of Philistines with a riddle only his wife could answer by tricking it out of him . . . or the brilliant King Solomon himself, who won the love of the equally brilliant Queen of Sheba in a Riddle Game that lasted for six long months. So you're too old for riddles." The Fool shrugged. "OK. Never mind, then."

They walked on.

"So what is it?" Sara asked.

"What is what?"

"What doesn't make you sad but always makes you cry?"

"I asked *you* that."

"Well, now I'm asking you."

"But you don't know the answer."

"So?"

"You can't ask a riddle you don't know the answer to yourself," the Fool said firmly. "It's against the rules."

"Riddles have rules?"

"Every game has rules. Every game worth playing."

"So what's the answer?"

"That's what I'm asking *you*," the Fool said.

"Well, I don't *know*, do I?"

"Ohhhhh!" The Fool acted like he'd just figured out something deep. "You give UP!"

It sounded a lot like losing a game, but she couldn't stand it any more. "Yeah, OK, I give up," Sara muttered. "Just tell me what it is."

"An onion."

Well, that was true. Sara's mother hated chopping onions because they not only made her cry, they also made her nose run.

"Now you tell me one," the Fool said.

"I don't know any."

"You don't—oh, Lord, give me patience. What do they do for fun in your world? Watch paint dry on the walls?"

"Watch TV."

"That's what I said!" She wished he didn't make her laugh. He was so annoying, she would have liked to be really mad at him. But there was something about his cheerful goodwill—even when he was teasing, she could tell he wanted to make her like him. And he was distracting her from worrying about the demons.

"So, all right, here's another one. This one's hard, but you're a bright girl. What flower stays green and fresh forever?"

"A rose?"

"You may be gifted, but you don't know much about flowers, do you? And don't say 'a plastic rose,' 'cause it doesn't count. What started out green, and stays green forever? Come on. . . ."

"A pine tree?"

He snorted. "What do you think this is, the Christmas Tree Shops? I said *flower*. You're not thinking."

Sara thought of all the flowers she knew. Didn't they all die eventually? "I give up."

"Love," said the Fool.

"*What?* That's not a flower!"

"It's a metaphor. The flower of love stays green and fresh forever—if you're lucky. If it's true love. You should be so lucky," he sighed. "We all should. So have you thought of one yet?"

Sara used to have a riddle book. She'd hide it in her desk at school and look at it when class got boring. It had pictures in it. She saw her favorite one now, so clearly she might have just been reading it behind her math book. And she bet it was one he didn't know. Sara said, "What key doesn't open a door?"

"A monkey."

"Nope."

"A turkey."

"Those aren't real kinds of keys. It has to be real."

"A fruit key."

"There's no such thing as a fruit key," Sara said— though for all she knew, there was here.

The Fool waved his arms in the air. "A key that you used to have the lock to but you lost when you moved across town and now you can't remember which door it went to and anyway the lock's all rusty?"

"Pathetic," Sara said. "Give up? Want me to tell you?" He nodded. "A piano key!"

He hit his own head. "Ouch! OK, listen: A man is sitting in a restaurant, a very busy restaurant. And every time the waiter rushes by, the man calls out, 'Waiter, waiter, taste this soup!' (He's got a bowl of soup in front of him, did I say that?)"

"What kind?"

"Pea soup—how should I know? Funny soup. It's a joke, so it's funny soup."

"Minestrone," said Sara. It was the funniest soup name she knew. Some people said *min-ess-TRO-nee* and some said *min-ess-TRONE*, which cracked her up either way.

"OK, minestrone," he said, doing the *TRO-nee*. "So: 'Waiter, waiter, taste this soup!' 'Just a minute, sir!' says the waiter. He is very busy. 'Waiter, waiter, taste this soup!' Finally, the waiter stops at the table. 'So where's the spoon?' he asks, and the man goes, 'A-HA!'"

Sara waited a moment. "That's it?"

"Don't you get it? The waiter never brought him a spoon! That was how he asked for it! Whatsamatter, don't they have restaurants where you come from?"

"Try another riddle," Sara said. (His riddles were better than his jokes.)

"What gets bigger the more you take out of it?"

"Love?"

"Hmm. Very philosophical. But no. You wouldn't let me have *monkey*, I'm not giving you *love*. So to speak. The more you take from it, the bigger it gets. What is it?"

Sara gave up.

"A hole in the ground."

The world changed around them with each joke the Fool told. Sometimes they were walking along a river, sometimes in a forest under trees. Sometimes the sky was blue, but once Sara thought she saw stars overhead. At least it never rained, though there were storm clouds as they crossed a little stone bridge. And then, suddenly, they were in the mountains. The purple mountains, Sara guessed, though once you were in them, they looked more grey than purple. They were on a narrow path, with rocks rising high on all sides of them. You couldn't really tell if it was day or night, the shadows were so deep.

The path stopped at a wall of solid rock.

"Uh-oh," said Sara, but the Fool said, "Finally!"

Sara looked up at the sheer rock face. It was so high it blotted out the sky. "Are we going to have to climb up this?" she asked nervously. "Do you know how? We did rope climbing in gym, but that's not the same thing, is it? Do you even have a rope? What if—"

"Hooooold your horses," said the Fool. "Do I detect a note of worry?"

"Well, it's just that if we have to climb it—"

"Climb it? Do I look like Sir Edmund Hillary to you?"

"Who's that?"

"'Who's that?' she asks me. What do they teach them nowadays? He climbed Mt. Everest. I don't look a thing like him, trust me. Get it?"

"OK. But how—"

"Get it?"

"I said OK. But—"

"No, no, nooooo," the Fool moaned. "When I say 'Get it?' you have to say 'Got it.' Try again. *Get it?*"

"Got it."

"Good." He nodded. "That's the ticket. Now, then, as to your cliff-climbing terrors, fear not, and also do not worry or be afraid. This is demon territory—everything's backward, remember? To go up—we go down. To go over, we go under. Jump!"

$\mathcal{S}$ARA JUMPED—just a little hop, really, to see what would happen.

What happened was that she felt herself falling, falling, like falling straight off a cliff. Her eyes were squeezed shut tight. Just when she was wondering if she should prepare for a crash landing, she felt herself slowing down. *It was like being a cartoon character,* Sara thought. But before she could try running her legs in circles in the air, she felt the ground softly meet her feet. She opened her eyes and saw the Fool floating gently down next to her.

His face was lit with orangey light by the torches burning all around them—torches held by demons of all shapes and sizes, some so funny-looking that Sara would have laughed if they weren't on a serious rescue mission.

Then one demon stepped forward, bigger than all the rest. His wings were shiny black, his eyes were red, and he had a huge, glittering crown on his head.

"Greetings, King Ashmedai!" said the Fool.

"Well, well," gloated the Demon King. Fire flickered in his nostrils. "So glad you decided to . . . drop in. We've been looking for a little entertainment."

"Then isn't this your lucky day—er, night? Entertainment is what we're all about. How'd you like us to do handstands for you?"

"Not that kind of entertainment. We were thinking more of something like . . . a little something called the Riddle Game."

"The Riddle Game, huh?" said the Fool. "Uh-oh. We don't know too many riddles, do we, Sara?"

"Oh, that's all right," the King said with oily happiness. "It's easy. And it's fun, too. Here's how it works: We ask you questions, and if you don't know the answers . . . we suck out your brains through a straw!"

"Sounds like a laugh riot," said Sara bravely. This wasn't getting them anywhere; they were here to rescue the dreydl, weren't they? And she did not want anyone sticking a straw anywhere near her brains, thank you very much. "But we have a question for you, first."

"That's not how it works," growled the Demon King. "*We* ask the questions. If you can answer all three, then you can ask us one. Whoever can't answer . . ." The King made a horrible slurping noise that seemed to go on forever. It was worse than her cousin Max finishing his chocolate milk when Aunt Rachel had been dumb enough to let him keep his straw. "It's lots of fun. You'll see."

The Fool said, "I guess we will."

"Are you ready? Then let's begin."

The demons started jumping up and down, cackling and giving the king advice. "I've got one! I've got one!"

"No, I know, I know!"

"Meeeee! Meeeeeeee!!!"

"Enough!" The King raised his scaly hand. His fingernails were painted a dark red, except the pinkies, which were blue and black. "Ornias shall speak the first riddle."

A demon with hair growing out in different-colored tufts in weird places all over his body stepped into the circle. Twisting horns sprang from his forehead. His legs ended in chicken feet—but the worst part was, they were on backward. Ornias was truly horrible to look at.

"Tremble, mortals," he said. ("Who are you calling a mortal, fuzzface?" muttered the Fool.) "For mine is a riddle so ancient that when Joseph was imprisoned in Egypt, he told it to his jailer to get extra pottage privileges. And now, here is my riddle. Listen well. *The more you take from me, the bigger I grow. What am I?*"

"A hole in the ground," Sara answered promptly.

"You knew it!" the King hissed.

"Not fair!" whined Ornias.

The Demon King hit Ornias on the head. "It is an old one," grumbled the King, "much too old. When Adam told it to Eve, she said she knew it already."

"The Fool has been around a long time; he probably heard it from Eve and told it to the girl," another demon said. This one was almost as round as a ball. When he

spoke, he swelled up, so that it looked as if he would burst right out of his greeny-purple skin. "But I will not fall into that same trap. I am the mighty Autothith, bringer of headaches and hangnails. I shall ask them something modern, something new. Something unheard of in the world until lately, such as even Reb Berele Berenson, the Laughing Rabbi of Schnitzelkov, could never have dreamed of on a night when he'd eaten five times his weight in creamed herring and washed it all down with peppermint brandy. Here is my riddle. Listen well. *What is it that is black and white . . . and yet is red all over?"*

The Fool opened his eyes wide. "Could it possibly be—an embarrassed zebra??"

"No!" Autothith cried. "It is . . . a newspaper!"

"I always heard 'an embarrassed zebra,'" Ornias muttered.

"Me, too."

"Penguin," another demon said. "An embarrassed penguin."

"Newspaper!" Autothith shrieked, getting even bigger. "Don't you get it?! *Red* all over—*read* all over?!!!"

"Calm down, Thith," the Demon King growled. "You'll give yourself a rupture. I don't want your slime all over the place again. Let us skip that one and ask another."

"But that's not fair," Sara said. "We gave a right answer. You can't ask us four riddles—it's not in the rules!"

"Foolish mortal!" laughed the Demon King. "What do you know of rules?"

"She's right," the Fool said quietly. "The game only works if you follow the rules. You know that, Ashmedai."

The Demon King kicked the ground. Dust rose up around him. "I don't care," he said. "I'm king. I make the rules around here."

"Yeah!" the other demons cried.

"Fine," said the Fool. He straightened the sock on his head. "Fine with us. Then we're not playing. C'mon, Sara, let's go."

"What do you mean you're not playing?" The Demon King shrieked so loudly Sara's ears hurt. "You have to play! We agreed! I was going to suck out your brains through a straw!"

"Three questions." The Fool looked over his shoulder.

"We got the first two right. You only get one more."

"One more!" the other demons were shouting. "We want more riddles!"

"Let it be so," Ashmedai said sulkily. "'Embarrassed zebra' will be accepted as the answer to the second question." Autothith started blowing himself up again. "Though 'a newspaper' would also have been correct," he hastened to add. "What does it matter? The final riddle is the hardest, and you will surely lose, for *I* will do the asking this time."

Sara looked at the Fool. So far so good, but what if he didn't know this one? What if it were really hard? Could they figure it out on their own? *Oh, stop worrying,* she told herself. *The demons aren't all that bright. It's probably just something dumb like, "Why did the chicken cross the road?"* She tried to think of all the riddles she knew, but her brain was being difficult, and all she could come up with was knock-knock jokes.

"Here is my riddle," said King Ashmedai. "Listen well. Ahem!" The demon cleared his throat. *"I have more eyes than you can count, but only two of them can see. What am I?"*

The Fool looked puzzled for once. Was there really one he didn't know? Sara bit her lip, thinking. She'd learned that all riddles made sense eventually. You just had to figure them out. Eyes that can't see . . . a potato? That has more eyes than you can count. But no, that wasn't the answer, not if two of them *can* see. What else has eyes? Eye of a daisy—was that real, or was she making it up? Eye of a storm . . . eye of a hurricane. What has two regular eyes and a bunch of eyes somewhere else . . . eyes in the back of their head? Eyes in their tail. . . . Of course.

"I've got it," Sara cried. "A peacock!"

"Curses," snarled the Demon King.

"Three!" shouted the Fool.

"Not fair!" the other demons whined, writhing and twisting themselves into even uglier shapes. They were such babies, Sara couldn't believe it.

"That was fun," the Fool said. "I guess it's our turn, now."

"All right," the King growled. "Ask me *one*. But tremble still, for I know the answer to all questions that ever were or will be."

Sara opened her mouth to ask about the dreydl, but the Fool put his finger on his lips in warning.

"I've got one," he said to the Demon King. "Ready? What looks like a box . . . smells like a lox . . . and flies?"

"Ohhh." The Demon King screwed his red eyes shut tight in thought. "A box? . . . It flies, you say? And it smells?"

"Like a lox. It's a kind of pickled fish, if that helps."

"It doesn't help! I know what lox is!"

"Then you give up?"

"No!"

But try as he might, the demon could not come up with an answer.

The stars wheeled in the sky.

"Look," said the Fool, "this is getting boring. Tell you what: if you give up, we won't suck your brains out through a straw. Instead, you agree to grant us one wish. How's that?"

"Oh, all right," growled the Demon King. "I do have the power to grant most wishes. What is it you want?"

The Fool looked at Sara and nodded. Sara stepped forward. "We want the Golden Dreydl!"

"Is that all?" The Demon King laughed. "No problem! We have plenty of golden dreydls here in our fortress. Come take a look! All the dreydls are dancing together right now. If you can find your friend, you can have her." The demons pranced about with their torches, all heading toward an enormous door in the side of the mountain. Sara and the Fool followed them in. The torches cast light and shadows up the walls, but the ceiling was so high it seemed to disappear in darkness above them. They were in a huge room carved out of the mountain's heart.

"How do you like it?" the Demon King's voice boomed.

Sara heard music, wonderful music that made her want to tap her toes to the beat. It made her want to swing and sway—it made her want to spin! The flickering torchlight made her feel a little dizzy. Maybe she should just follow the music. . . .

"Hey, Sara!" She felt the Fool's hand on her wrist. "What key doesn't open a door?"

She looked at his pale face and realized he was sending her a message: *Don't get sucked into the demons' world. Remember who you are, or we'll never get out of here.*

"Get it?" the Fool said.

"Got it."

"Good! So what is it?"

Again the picture from her old riddle book was before her, silly and black-and-white, funny and sharp, not at all like the twisting demon music. . . .

"A piano key." She felt her head clear a little.

"You're good at riddles, you know that, kid? That peacock answer—pure genius. Which is good, because I think we've just fallen into another kind of riddle. And I, for one, am not sure I get it this time."

Sara looked down, and then around the hall. She knew exactly what he meant. The place was full of dreydls, dozens and dozens of them. And all of them were golden, just like her special gift.

"That does it," said the Fool. "We'll never find the right one."

"Silence!" roared the Demon King. "The girl asked. The girl must choose."

All the dreydls were spinning round and round the floor in crazy patterns, bumping into each other and spinning away, but never falling down.

"Pretty, aren't they?" Ashmedai gloated. "We could watch them for hours. They never change. They never fall over. I think they're just perfect, don't you?"

Sara just gazed at the dreydls, feeling a little sick.

"Only one is the dreydl you seek," Ashmedai taunted. "You have to pick right the first time. You don't get a second chance in *this* game. If you choose the wrong one, you'll have to join them in their little dance—like the rest of the poor fools who tried to defeat us. We'll have two nice, new, shiny dreydls to play with—and you'll be spinning with them—forever!"

Where had all these poor people come from? Suddenly, Sara was afraid she knew. The Queen of Sheba and her caravan had been hurrying to rescue the dreydl princess. But the demons must have gotten them first. Now here they were, all spinning away with enchantment . . . and all exactly the same.

"Don't give up," the Fool said nervously. "There *must* be a way!"

"Let me see." Sara stared into the crowd. "My dreydl had a scratch on her arm—we just have to find one with the scratch on it."

"How can you tell? They're all going so fast."

"Hold still," Sara begged the dizzying dancers. "Oh, please hold still, just for a second."

But the dreydls never stopped. If one had a scratch, it blurred into the spinning dance. Round and round their four sides went, round and round went the magical Hebrew letters. . . .

"Give up," Ashmedai gloated. The other demons laughed. "Why don't you just give up and join them? Isn't the music pretty? All they have to do is spin and be admired."

"Sara—" warned the Fool, but Sara wasn't even listening to the demons anymore. She was staring hard at the dreydls, willing her eyes to see through the blur of movement.

"Hold it," said Sara. "The letters—they're all backward!"

"You're right! When the demons copied the real dreydl, they put the letters on the wrong way! So instead of *nun, gimel, hey* and *shin,* they're . . ."

"Don't even say it; it's making me dizzy!"

"You'll be dizzier before we're through, if you don't

pick the right one. Look for the one with the letters going the right way! Concentrate!"

"Give up?" came the Demon King's mocking laughter.

At the sound, one of the dreydls wobbled, just a little. In that tiny moment, Sara saw the scratch on its side—and then she read the letters: *nun, gimel, hey, shin*.

"That one!" she shouted, pointing.

"*Nooooo!!*" wailed the demons—but it was too late. All around them, the enchanted dreydls were changing back to people—tall and short, skinny and fat, young and old. (Sara was relieved not to see the Queen of Sheba there. But of course she realized the queen had powerful magic. She'd probably gotten away in time.) And there among them was Sara's own golden-haired friend, her hair even wilder and frizzier than ever.

"You did it, Sara!" cried the dreydl girl. "You rescued us all!" She gave Sara a big hug, and Sara hugged her back. "I am soooo glad to see you! I love to spin, but spinning forever with no chance to fall down . . ." The girl shuddered. "It's like nothing could ever change."

"Boring," said Sara.

"Scary," said the girl.

The Fool bowed to her. "Greetings, Daughter of Solomon."

"Oh, hi there," she grinned at him. "How've you been? And how's your flying lox box?"

"*Flying lox box?!!?*" screamed the Demon King. "*That* was the answer?!"

The Fool shrugged. "It always was, it always has been, and it always will be."

Ashmedai's face was turning as red as his nails. Flames shot out of his nose. "That's the stupidest riddle I ever heard."

"Cheer up," said the Fool. "Next time someone asks you, you'll know the answer."

"I hate that riddle," the King hissed.

"Me, too," growled Ornias.

"Yeahhhh," whispered Autothith.

"This," said the Fool, "may be the worst audience I've ever had, and I've had a few. I haven't had so much trouble with a crowd since I *tummled* the wedding of Jacob and Leah. Now, *that* was a disaster!"

The demons were getting ugly. Sara was twisting her fingers with worry. "Out," she said. "Now."

The Fool looked up from his memories. "You think? But things are just getting interesting."

She was about to ask what his idea of interesting was when she found out. There was a brilliant flash of light, green as new leaves, and light filled the cavern, soft and bright as the morning after a storm. She heard a voice, coming from nowhere and everywhere, speaking words she couldn't understand . . . but she felt a thrill run through her, as if she'd been asleep and had just woken up. Everything looked sharp and clear. The people who had been enchanted were clustered together, blinking and smiling and touching each other as if they couldn't believe it. The demons were gnashing their teeth and waving their arms about and trying to run backward and running into walls. As soon as each demon touched a wall, he seemed to stick to it—and slowly to become part of it. It was as if the rock were water and each demon was sinking down, down, down—or maybe becoming part of the rock itself.

King Ashmedai spread his huge wings and tried to spring at Sara and her friends. But a voice rang out in the clear air: "Be thou bound, Ashmedai and all thy minions of mischief and mayhem, now and forever!" And the

Demon King was sucked backward through the air into the rock, where he hung high up like a particularly large and ugly sculpture.

"I'll be baaaaaaaaaaaack!" she heard Ashmedai wail.

"I doubt that," said the Fool.

Sara and her friends watched as the last of the demons disappeared into the wall of the huge cavern.

"Solomon has spoken the Word of Binding. And this time it will not be undone. For the four letters have returned to us here.

"Now, come," the Fool continued, beckoning to the princess, "spin your letters for us, Daughter of Solomon, and bring us to the Tree of Life."

"Do I really have to?" the dreydl princess asked. "To tell you the truth, I'm a little sick of spinning right now."

"This is different," said the Fool. "The demons tied up your power; this releases it—and gets us there faster, too. Get it?"

The dreydl princess nodded. "Got it."

"Good."

She raised her hands above her head and began to turn. "But spin with me, will you?"

"Is it part of the magic?" Sara asked.

"No." Her voice came from the center of spinning gold that was her hair. "But it's fun!"

Sara started spinning, too. She closed her eyes and went round and round and round. She didn't feel dizzy. She just felt free.

Chapter 9

"Oof!" The dreydl princess fell down on the grass, and Sara fell all tangled up with her, still laughing. It was daylight, and they were someplace else, someplace different, green and beautiful and new.

The Fool looked on anxiously. "What is the letter you landed on, Princess?" he asked. "What is our fate?"

She looked down, and drew a deep breath. "*Gimel,*" said the dreydl girl. "We win!"

Sara heard cheering. She looked up to see a crowd of happy faces: all the people they'd rescued from the demons, yes—but also the Queen of Sheba, with all her camels. At the queen's side stood a tall man with a flowing black beard and curls, robed in purple and crowned in gold: King Solomon in all his glory.

The royal couple stood together under a tall, spreading cedar tree. When the dreydl girl saw them, she gave a joyful cry and ran to her parents' arms.

The Queen of Sheba kissed her over and over. "Welcome back, my child. Goodness, how you've grown! What's this scratch on your arm? Look at your hair, what a mess. . . . Oh, sweetness!"

King Solomon held her close. "My daughter," he said. "You have returned to us, and just in time. For see, above us, how the Tree of Life grows faint. Its branches droop, its needles fade, and the sap runs weak in it."

The princess nodded. "I'm sorry," she said. "I didn't

mean to stay away so long. I didn't mean to get captured by the demons, either. Things just kept happening to me."

Solomon nodded. "That is the way of the world. But you are here now, and it is time for you to fulfill your destiny." He lifted his hands over her head. "Now I call on the four powerful letters I invested in you to rise and manifest their power: the power of Knowledge, the power of Strength of Heart, the power of Mercy, the power of Lovingkindness! With these letters, dance now, my daughter, dance around the Tree, and give it life for us and all the world!"

The princess tilted back her golden head, looking up at the branches above her and the sky above them. She put up first one arm, and then the other, and her feet took one step and then another. Sometimes with her back to the tree, sometimes facing it, she turned about the majestic cedar's trunk. She seemed to be weaving a golden rope. Her hair whipped out behind her as she danced faster and faster . . . and her dance became the spinning of a top, too big for a child to hold, a tiny sun whirling through space.

Around and around the tree she went, and Sara imagined she saw her leaving a trail of burning letters in her wake: *Nun, gimel, hey, shin . . . Nes Gadol Haya Sham:* A Great Miracle Was There.

As the princess danced, the tree seemed to breathe. Its boughs grew stronger and straighter, and the green of its canopy nearly filled the sky. At last the golden-haired girl fell, breathless and glowing, back against the tree's enormous trunk. For a moment, the tree seemed to bend and embrace her. Then a great stillness filled the land.

King Solomon placed his hand on his daughter's brow, and then on her temples, and then on her heart. "It is finished," he said. "The binding of the magic is complete. My daughter is restored to us, and the Tree of Life is safe."

The Fool winked at Sara. "Let's do handstands," said the Fool. But Sara shook her head, no. It wasn't the time for being foolish for her.

"What's the matter?" the Fool asked. "You're the heroine, you should be happy."

"That doesn't count," Sara said sadly. "It's over, I know it. In all the stories, that's how it goes. I finished my quest: I rescued the dreydl princess with the help of some magical friends, and now I just have to go home. Those are the rules, it's how it works."

"What's wrong with going home?"

She tried to knuckle a tear back into her eye. "You don't understand. I'm in so much trouble there. I fought with my brother and all the cousins at a family party, and we broke—I broke the TV. . . . Everyone hates me. It's so bad I don't even know what my punishment will be. And it's not like I can tell anyone what really happened! Nobody will ever know about the d-dreydl, because I can't tell them about this or they'd think I was crazy, not anyone at all, ever. . . ."

"Not anyone?" Sara heard a friendly voice. Turning around, she saw a woman dressed in royal robes of silk. Her long, white hair fell curling down her proud shoulders like a waterfall, and her face shone with light. But there was something familiar about her. . . .

"Tante Miriam?!"

"You were expecting maybe Barbie? Of course it's me." Tante Miriam held out her arms, and Sara ran to them. Tante Miriam might look like a queen, but it was definitely the same old lady who had appeared, all raggedy and travel-worn, at the family party. She was family, too, and she was here.

"Oh, my Sara . . ." Tante Miriam hugged her close, and her voice was as warm as her arms, saying, "Sara, my darling. Such a girl, such a daughter of Israel, such a treasure, such a jewel . . ."

For some reason, it was her warmth that made Sara cry, deep sobs that melted into her auntie's gown as she held her.

"It's all right," Tante Miriam murmured into her hair. "Really, really it is. I chose you for the Golden Dreydl and the Golden Dreydl for you *because* of who you are, not in

spite of it. I chose you for your stubbornness and your good sense and your curiosity and your kindness. And I chose well."

Sara sniffled.

Tante Miriam handed her a silk handkerchief. "Oh, and listen, don't worry—I used to fight with my brother, too."

"You did?" Sara raised her face.

"Of course I did. And he was a lot bigger than yours, and very important. We had some pretty great fights, my brother and I. But even Moses sometimes listened to me."

"My lady." It was the Fool addressing Tante Miriam. Her aunt nodded to him, wiped Sara's face, and led her forward to where the king stood under the tree.

"Welcome, Sara, our great friend, our rock, and our helper," said King Solomon.

Her dreydl friend put her arm around her. "Isn't she the greatest?"

The king smiled. "Without you, none of this would have been possible. Without you, our daughter could not have crossed back between the worlds."

Did he mean it was good that she'd broken the TV screen? *Oh, boy,* Sara sighed. She wondered if Tante

Miriam was going to show up there again to explain it all to the family. Somehow, she doubted it.

"Without you," the king went on, "our child would have had no friend to help her. Without you, she could never have been set free." Was he done now? This was getting embarrassing. Everyone was standing there in a big circle admiring her, and she found she just wanted to hide. She should do something, she knew, but she didn't know what. She didn't know how to curtsy, or make speeches, or do magic. A handstand was starting to seem like a good idea. Did King Solomon like jokes? She looked at the crowd. The Fool made an unbelievably goofy face at her, and Tante Miriam gave her the thumbs-up sign, and she found the nerve to answer, "I didn't do much, great king."

"Your help was timely and good. Accept our thanks, and those of all who dwell here."

The people started cheering. This wasn't so bad. Sara found herself grinning.

"Sa-*ra!* Sa-*ra!*" her dreydl friend shouted. The Fool was doing cartwheels, and Tante Miriam was waving her scarf like a flag. Sara waved back. Finally, things quieted down.

"I know you must return to your own home now," said the king, "but before you go, name your reward. If it is within my power, you shall have it."

The thought of home brought her quickly back to earth. It was going to be awful. Unless—"Can you fix it so the TV's not broken any more?"

"Of course," the king said with a smile. "But let me give you something else, as well: a blessing on your courage and your wisdom, for both have served us well this day, and we are grateful."

King Solomon raised his hands high over his head, his fingers spread out over her. "As you read the letters right, and knew truth from falsehood, so you will always be able to distinguish between them. You will live and grow, and the letters will dance for you!"

The letters seemed to be dancing right now: Sara saw them all going around the tree in a golden blur—not just the letters of the dreydl, but every letter of the alphabet, combining to make word after word as they danced, as if the world itself were being created in letters—or maybe it was the people she had rescued, dancing in their joy, dancing because they could choose to dance as they would wish, instead of being forced to spin for no reason.

Sara found herself caught up in the dance, with the Fool on one side, and a small warm hand that could only be the Golden Dreydl's. Sara seemed to be melting into the golden light like butter . . . light was in her eyes, warmth on her face. . . .

Chapter 10

SARA! HEY, SARA!"

Cousin Amy was flapping the window shade, letting morning light flood across the bed. "Are you getting up or what? Breakfast's cooking!"

Sara smelled the rich golden scent of melted butter and frying batter wafting through the door.

"We're having pancakes—hurry up!"

She unwound herself from the tangle of sheets and knuckled her eyes. She felt soft cloth rubbing them. It was a silk handkerchief, still clutched in her fist. Tante Miriam's handkerchief.

She stuffed it in the pocket of her pajamas and went down to join the family.

After breakfast, when the dishes were all washed and everyone was dressed, the kids were allowed into the living room to play with the presents they seemed to have opened the night before. Everyone agreed that Tante Miriam's were the best (everyone except the people who were going to have to listen to Cousin Jonathan hammering on his new frame drum for months to come, or Max shouting, "Aye, aye, me hearties!" all day and whining about why he couldn't have a parrot). Then Amy and Jason got into a tussle over her telescope, because Amy wanted to look up the chimney with it, but Jason wanted to spy on the neighbors across the street.

"Whoaaaa!" Uncle Izzy lifted it right out of their hands. "Careful where you point that thing! You nearly cracked the television."

There was the huge screen, in perfect shape, good as new.

Well, if you could bind demons to rock without even touching them, Sara thought, *I guess you would be able to fix a busted TV, too.*

She looked under a few chairs for her golden dreydl, but she didn't think she'd find it.

"Get packed, kids," their mother told them. "We've got to get home this afternoon. Don't forget your toothbrush again, Sara—oh, and don't forget to pack your fan!"

"Fan?" Sara asked.

"Your present Tante Miriam gave you, darling—the peacock feather fan. I don't know why she thought you needed one, but that's just the way she is. I guess you can hang it on the wall or something. . . ."

"Oh, right," said Sara, laughing, "*that* present!"

Of course the Golden Dreydl was nowhere to be found. And neither was Tante Miriam.

Nobody had seen her leave. "She's just like that," said Sara's mother later in the car going home. "She never stays anywhere for long. She never calls, and she never writes. She just turns up when she feels like it."

"Cool," said Seth. "Hey, Sara, do you have any chocolate left?"

"Yep," she said. "And, no, you can't have any. It's not my fault you ate all yours. Move over. You're taking all the room."

"I need more, I'm bigger than you."

"Tough luck."

"You can each have exactly half the backseat," their mother said firmly. "Those are the rules, and the rules don't change."

Sara smiled.

"Hey, Seth," she said. "What looks like a box, smells like a lox, and flies?"

"Is that a riddle?" said Seth. He'd loved riddles ever since he'd read *The Hobbit*. "Give me a minute."

But he never got it, and she made him wait a long time before she'd tell him the answer.

Glossary

Phrases in Languages Spoken by Jews Around the World

Buen moed (Ladino): Good (happy) holiday

Gut yomtov (Yiddish): Good (happy) holiday

Hag sameach (Hebrew): Happy holiday

Hanuka alegre (Ladino): Happy Chanukah

Tante (Yiddish): Aunt

Chanukah (Hebrew): A Jewish holiday that celebrates the victory of the heroic Maccabees against the wicked Syrian king who was trying to make the Jews give up their religion and be just like everyone else in his empire. Also known as the "Festival of Lights," Chanukah is celebrated for eight days in December. It can also be spelled Hanukkah.

Dreydl (Yiddish): A four-sided top that people play with during Chanukah. It can also be spelled dreidel, dreidl, or even draydel.

Kiddush cup (Hebrew/English): A special fancy cup for wine that is used on holidays and on Shabbat when a blessing (called "kiddush") is said over the wine.

Ladino: A language spoken by Sephardic Jews, a mix of Hebrew and medieval Spanish. Its roots are in the language spoken by the Jews of Spain who were expelled from the country in 1492. They fled throughout the Mediterranean area, settling in Turkey and other Middle

Eastern countries, as well as in the Balkans, Italy, and southern France.

LATKES (YIDDISH): Fried potato pancakes, a special Chanukah treat.

MENORAH (HEBREW): A candelabra, or holder for candles, that has seven branches for seven candles. The special one used for Chanukah is also called a chanukiah. It has eight branches for eight candles, one for each of the eight days of Chanukah, plus a ninth holder for the "servant" candle that lights all the others.

RABBI (HEBREW): The religious leader of the congregation of a synagogue or temple, who leads the service on the Sabbath and on holidays. The rabbi is also a teacher who studies and interprets Jewish law.

SANDY KOUFAX: A great Jewish baseball player known as "the man with the golden arm." Now in the Baseball Hall of Fame, he broke records pitching for the Brooklyn Dodgers. When the 1965 World Series fell on Yom

Kippur, the holiest day of the Jewish year, he chose not to play rather than break the sanctity of the day.

SHABBAT (HEBREW): Saturday, the seventh day of the Jewish week, when God rested after creating the world. Jewish people are supposed to rest on this day, and many go to religious services.

TORAH (HEBREW): A parchment scroll on which are handwritten the first five books of the Bible. Torahs are kept in a special place in the synagogue, called the ark, and are dressed in beautifully decorated coverings. During Shabbat services the Torah is taken out and paraded around the synagogue, and a different section is read aloud each week.

TUMMLER (YIDDISH): An entertainer who keeps things lively and makes sure everyone is involved in the joy and silliness of a party.

YIDDISH: A language spoken by Ashkenazic Jews, a mix of Hebrew and (mostly medieval) German. Many

American Jews have grandparents and great-grandparents who spoke only Yiddish when they came to this country from Russia and Eastern Europe, and many Yiddish words have entered the English language.

YINGLISH: A mixture of Yiddish and English marked by borrowings from both languages.

Thank You

WHEN I WAS THIRTEEN it took me more than six months to write all the thank-you notes for my bat mitzvah presents, and I have the awful feeling there is still someone I missed. I'm trying never again to miss thanking someone who gave me something nice, so here goes.

Thank you to:

The guys of Shirim, a wonderful klezmer band in Boston, who inspired me with their recording, *Klezmer Nutcracker*... band leader Glenn Dickson and keyboard wizard Michael McLaughlin, who helped me create a story to go with their klezmer music . . . my friends at WGBH and PRI radio stations, who were with me all the way, especially Jon Solins, Helen Barrington, Jeffrey Nelson, and Gary Mott—then along came Judy O'Malley, an editor worth waiting for. To her and all the good people of Charlesbridge, and especially the illustrator, Ilene Winn-Lederer, my sincere thanks for making this the book you hold in your hands.

I got extra help from the Shahan Bromberg family, especially Liran and Aliza. Delia Sherman, Holly Black, Cassandra Claire, and Deborah Manning turned a little of their wisdom my way.

Most of all, I want to thank all of the kids who have come to my stage performances with Shirim of *The Golden Dreydl*, who have laughed, clapped, riddled, and danced. You make the magic live. Keep spinning!

Did I leave anyone out? Tell you what: I'll write you a personal note. And this time my mom won't have to remind me. (Oh, hi, Mom. Thanks for all of your help with the glossary. *Phew!*)